SUNNY DAYS AND RAIN

A PLAY BY

JASON E. WEBER

CHARACTERS

COLIN – A fourteen year old boy

ROSS – Colin's best friend

BRIGID – Ross' girlfriend

KATY – A new friend

A NOTE ON STAGING

The staging of this play can be as realistic as feasible. If the funds permitted, a realistic bridge could span the stage as foliage peeked in from the wings. However, the play is written to be intensely character driven. Whatever the set is, it should not take away from the emotion in the play. To that end, it may be more beneficial for the set to be merely an elevated platform. That said, any set within that range can be appropriate. This play, therefore, can easily accommodate any size theatre.

ACT ONE

Scene 1

Nearly midnight on the last day of summer, two fourteen year-old boys, COLIN and ROSS sit on a dilapidated railroad bridge staring at the river below. All of the scenes take place on this same bridge.

Colin spits.

Silence.

COLIN: I'd say about three seconds.

ROSS: I got two.

   (*Colin spits again.*)

COLIN: Maybe it is two.

ROSS: How about two and a half?

COLIN: Two and a half?

ROSS: (*shrugging*) I don't know. (*getting an idea*) Let me try. You
    count.

COLIN: Okay.

   (*Ross spits.*)

ROSS: Well?

COLIN: Three.

ROSS: You sure?

COLIN: I think so.

(*They look down at the river. Pause.*)

ROSS: (*looking to Colin*) So, what does it mean?

COLIN: (*looking to Ross*) Huh?

ROSS: How tall is the bridge?

COLIN: Oh. (*honestly*) I don't know.

ROSS: (*confused*) I thought you said you could figure it out.

COLIN: I said I saw them do it on TV.

ROSS: So, you don't know how?

COLIN: (*matter-of-fact*) No. Not really.

ROSS: Oh.

   (*They look back at the river. Pause.*)

COLIN: If I had to guess, I'd say it's about twenty feet.

ROSS: To the water?

COLIN: Yeah. Twenty feet to the water.

ROSS: (*looking to Colin*) How deep you think the water is?

COLIN: (*still watching the river.*) I don't know. Five?

ROSS: You think?

COLIN: (*looking to Ross*) I don't know, probably. It isn't that deep.

ROSS: I'd say less.

COLIN: (*looking to the river*) It's hard to tell. You can't see the
   bottom.

ROSS: It's dark out.

COLIN: (*looking to Ross*) Well, even during the day you can't.

ROSS: I guess.

   (*Back to the river. Pause.*)

   So about twenty-five feet then?

COLIN: Yeah. Seems right.

ROSS: (*standing*) That's one heck of a drop.

COLIN: (*looking to Ross*) It's not too bad.

ROSS: It'd still kill you, ya know.

COLIN: You think?

ROSS: Yeah. Twenty-five feet, only five feet of water. (*scoffs*) That's suicide.

COLIN: I betcha you could survive that.

ROSS: (*unsure*) Maybe.

COLIN: There's only one way to find out.

(*He gestures to Ross to give it a try.*)

ROSS: Me?

COLIN: Yeah, you. Give it a whirl.

ROSS: Why me?

COLIN: 'Cause you are the disbeliever.

(*Ross gives Colin a look.*)

ROSS: (*confidently*) Okay. Fine, I'll do it.

(*He moves toward the edge, takes a deep breath, and puts his arms over his head like a diver.*)

COLIN: (*with a smile*) Knock it off.

ROSS: Nope. It's gotta be tested.

(*Ross bends his knees.*)

COLIN: (*more serious*) Ross, don't.

ROSS: (*standing again*) Oh, not so confident now, eh?

(*Colin eyes Ross.*)

COLIN: (*cooly*) Fine. Jump if you want.

(*Ross hits him playfully in the arm.*)

What?

ROSS: (*backing down*) You would let me drown.

COLIN: Oh, never.

ROSS: Please.

COLIN: I woulda jumped in right after you.

ROSS: That's the biggest lie I ever heard.

COLIN: I never lie.

ROSS: Bullshit. Besides, you can't even swim.

COLIN : Do you think I would let a little thing like that stop me from saving my only best friend?

ROSS: Yes.

COLIN: (*reconsidering*) Well, maybe.

(*They laugh. Ross walks away. Colin spits. Pause.*)

Can you believe summer's over already?

ROSS: No. (*pointedly*) I swear it was shorter this year. I tell you, they're trying to screw us out of our time off. It's a conspiracy!

COLIN: (*smirking*) Totally.

(*Pause. Colin breaks off a piece of wood and tosses it into the river.*)

(*more serious*) Hey, Ross.

ROSS: Yeah, man?

COLIN: Are you—?

(*Pause.*)

ROSS: Am I what?

COLIN: Nevermind.

ROSS: No, what?

COLIN: Forget it.

ROSS: Colin.

COLIN: (*a little snappy*) I said nevermind, okay?

ROSS: Okay.

(*Silence.*)

Did you go school shopping yet?

COLIN: Yeah. My mom took me today.

ROSS: Mine too. (*sitting up*) Didn't you think it was weird to do it without a list?

COLIN: A list?

ROSS: You know, the school-approved school supply list.

COLIN: Oh. Yeah. It was.

ROSS: My mom kept asking if I needed anything special, and I kept saying, "I don't know." 'Cause I didn't.

COLIN: Right.

ROSS: I hope I got the right stuff. I don't wanna have to go through that again.

COLIN: That bad?

ROSS: Shopping with my mother? Yeah. She's crazy.

COLIN: (*laughing*) She is.

ROSS: Did I tell you what I got though?

COLIN: Nu-uh.

ROSS: (*really excited*) I got these super cool hologram folders.

COLIN: What?

ROSS: They're just like normal folders, right? But they have these pictures of space shuttles on the fronts, and when you hold them a certain way the space shuttle totally looks 3D. It's so awesome.

COLIN: (*skeptical*) Neat.

ROSS: (*still excited*) It is! I'll have to show them to you at school on Monday.

COLIN: Yeah. At school.

(*Colin breaks off another piece of wood and throws it in the river. Ross moves to sit next to Colin.*)

ROSS: What's wrong, man?

COLIN: What?

ROSS: What's wrong? You seem droopy.

COLIN: Oh. Nothing, I'm fine.

ROSS: Colin, I know you better than that.

COLIN: I'm fine.

ROSS: You sure?

COLIN: Yeah... It's just that— nevermind.

ROSS: Come on, Col. Lay it on me.

COLIN: I don't know.

ROSS: Colin.

COLIN: (*mocking*) Ross.

ROSS: Just tell me.

COLIN: Fine. (*with difficulty*) I don't think I'm ready.

ROSS: Ready for what?

COLIN: High School.

ROSS: What?

COLIN: (*unsure*) Well— I'm scared.

ROSS: Scared?

COLIN: (*retreating*) Well, not scared, just— worried. You know?

ROSS: Oh, come on, man. You'll be fine. You're like the smartest kid I know.

COLIN: It's not that.

ROSS: Then what is it?

COLIN: (*sheepishly*) It's just— I'm nervous... (*opening up*) Okay, fine. I am scared.

ROSS: Of what?

COLIN: Everything! The students, the teachers, the building. That's a huge building.

ROSS: They have maps.

COLIN: A school shouldn't need maps.

ROSS: But it has 'em.

COLIN: A school shouldn't be that big. I'm so gonna get lost.

ROSS: Colin.

COLIN: I'll probably end up in some uncharted corner.

ROSS: Colin.

COLIN: Die of starvation because I can't find the cafeteria.

ROSS: Colin!

COLIN: What?

ROSS: Calm down.

COLIN: I am calm!

ROSS: (*smiling*) You aren't.

COLIN: You're right. I'm freaking out! I can't do this. Why can't they just tack on grades to middle school? Why can't things just stay the way they are? I like the way they are!

ROSS: It's part of life, man. It's part of growing up.

COLIN: It bites.

ROSS: Yeah. Well. It's not gonna be all bad.

COLIN: Yes, it is.

ROSS: (*smirking*) It won't. There'll be good parts.

COLIN: Like what?

ROSS: Like, um... They'll be a whole mess of new people to meet.

COLIN: I hate meeting new people. I suck at it.

ROSS: Everyone does.

COLIN: You don't. You remember when we went to camp last summer?

ROSS: Yeah. What about it?

COLIN: After the first day, you were friends with practically everyone.

ROSS: I wasn't.

COLIN: Yeah, you were. You did that stupid impression of the one counselor, and everyone loved you.

ROSS: You talk like didn't have any friends there.

COLIN: I didn't. Just you.

ROSS: What about Billy Triviani?

COLIN: Who?

ROSS: He had the bunk bed next to yours.

COLIN: He wasn't my friend. He was your friend.

ROSS: He was your friend too. Don't you remember sneaking out to raid the kitchen with him?

COLIN: Yeah. But he never talked to me. He only talked to you.

ROSS: He talked to you.

COLIN: No. He never did. Just you.

ROSS: I don't remember that.

COLIN: It happened.

ROSS: He totally talked to you too.

(Colin holds his head.)

COLIN: Gah! High school's gonna suck so much. I should just drop out now.

ROSS: Like that would go over well with your mother.

COLIN: Screw my mother.

ROSS: Ew, no thank you.

COLIN: (giving him a look) You know what I mean.

ROSS: I know. I do. (beat) Look, high school's not gonna be as bad as you are making it out to be. I mean, I'll be right there with you the whole time. We've gotten through tough things before, right?

(Colin doesn't answer.)

Right?

COLIN: I guess.

ROSS: (more persistent) Right?

COLIN: (laughing) Yeah.

ROSS: What's so funny?

COLIN: I just remembered the time that we got locked in the walk-in cooler at your dad's store.

ROSS: Oh geez.

COLIN: That was awesome.

ROSS: It was awful.

COLIN: We had to pick the lock from the inside.

ROSS: If I remember correctly, you were the one that got it open.

COLIN: Using the paper clips you found in the back of the cooler.

ROSS: (*smiling*) Right, right.

(*They laugh.*)

Man, I thought we were gonna die in there.

COLIN: Me too.

ROSS: But we made it out.

(*Pause.*)

COLIN: I guess that makes us a pretty good team.

ROSS: I would say so.

(*Pause.*)

COLIN: I still can't believe you got us locked in there

ROSS: Me?

COLIN: Yeah. You. You let the door close.

ROSS: I beg to differ my friend.

(*Their conversation trails out as the lights fade to black.*)

Scene 2

Late Afternoon two weeks later, ROSS and COLIN are doing homework. Their backpacks, textbooks, notebooks, and folders are spread out around them.

ROSS: (*looking up from his notebook*) Hey, Col.

COLIN: (*not looking up*) Yeah?

ROSS: You got anything to eat?

COLIN: Nope.

  (*Silence. Ross reads for a bit then calls to Colin again.*)

ROSS: Colin.

COLIN: (*still not looking up*) Yeah?

ROSS: Did you see that booger hanging out of Mr. Krakauer's nose today?

COLIN: That's sounds disgusting.

  (*Pause.*)

ROSS: It was pretty awesome.

COLIN: (*looking up now*) So, how's the homework coming?

ROSS: Oh. Great. Great. I'm on number... uh... two.

COLIN: Ross, there's twenty-five problems.

ROSS: So?

COLIN: We've been out here for an hour.

ROSS: So? What number you on?

COLIN: Eighteen.

ROSS: Wow, you're quick.

COLIN: No. I just don't stop to ask for food every five minutes.

ROSS: It's not my fault that I'm hungry. My mom made meatloaf for dinner. That shit's inedible.

COLIN: I always liked your mom's meatloaf.

ROSS: That's 'cause you're a kiss-ass.

COLIN: (*crumpling and throwing a blank sheet of notebook paper at him*) Screw you.

ROSS: Aw, truth hurts, don't it?

(*Colin sets his books down and dives after Ross.*)

COLIN: Shut up!

ROSS: Colin's a kiss-ass!

COLIN: (*getting Ross in a headlock*) Take it back!

ROSS: You can't make me.

COLIN: (*tightening the headlock*) Watch me!

ROSS: Colin!

COLIN: Take it back.

ROSS: Colin, stop. That hurts!

COLIN: Take it back!

ROSS: Fine, fine! I take it back!

(*Colin lets go.*)

Someone can't take a joke.

(*Colin shoves Ross.*)

COLIN: (*smiling*) Shut up.

(*Colin walks away, nearly stepping on one of Ross' folders.*)

ROSS: Hey! Watch it!

COLIN: What?

ROSS: You almost stepped on my folder.

COLIN: (*sitting down with his work*) Oh, sorry.

ROSS: (*testing the folder*) You coulda messed up the hologram.

COLIN: (*not concerned*) Did I?

ROSS: (*examining it*) No. It looks okay. (*getting lost in the image*) Man, that's so cool. (*holding it out*) Hey, Col, did I show you this one?

COLIN: You showed me all of them.

ROSS: But what about this one? I'm not sure I showed you this one.

COLIN: You did.

ROSS: You didn't even look at it.

COLIN: I saw it already.

ROSS: Come on, just take a look.

COLIN: Okay, fine. Give it to me.

   (*He takes it and looks.*)

   (*sarcastically*) Ooo... neat. It looks so real.

ROSS: Give it back.

COLIN: (*mocking him*) I'd like to, but I can't. I'm too mesmerized by the image.

ROSS: Shut up.

COLIN: I feel like I can just reach out and touch the astronaut.

   (*He tries to put is hand "into" the picture*)

ROSS: Stop being a jerk.

   (*he takes the folder back.*)

   I think they're cool.

COLIN: (*going back to his homework*) They are.

   (*Ross stares at the folder for awhile. He gets lost in the image. Colin looks up and sees Ross.*)

   Hey.

   (*No response.*)

   Ross.

   (*No response. Colin crumples up another sheet of paper and throws it at Ross.*)

Earth to Ross!

ROSS: Hey man! What gives?

COLIN: You went into a fog.

ROSS: What?

COLIN: You were staring at your folder. I thought the astronaut was sucking your brains out.

ROSS: Funny. (*looking again at the folder*) I was just thinking.

COLIN: About?

ROSS: I don't know. You'll think it's stupid.

COLIN: No I won't.

ROSS: You will. (with disdain) My dad does.

COLIN: Do I look like your Dad?

ROSS: A little.

(*Colin goes to crumple another piece of paper.*)

(*stopping him*) Just kidding.

COLIN: So, what were you thinking about?

ROSS: What do you wanna be when you grow up?

COLIN: I don't know.

ROSS: Haven't you ever even thought about it?

COLIN: No, not really. (*off-hand*) My dad used to work at the car factory before he died. That doesn't sound too bad.

ROSS: The car factory?

COLIN: Yeah. It seems like a good job.

ROSS: Seems boring.

COLIN: Well, it's work.

ROSS: Don't you ever want some excitement.

COLIN: Sure, I guess. Why? What do you wanna be?

ROSS : You're gonna laugh.

COLIN: I said I wouldn't. Just tell me.

ROSS: I don't know

COLIN: Come on, man, it's me.

ROSS: Oh, yeah sure. Like that means you won't laugh.

COLIN: Show a little faith.

ROSS: Fine. (*with difficulty*) I wanna be an astronaut.

COLIN: (*with a smile*) An astronaut.

ROSS: See! You're gonna laugh!

COLIN: Am I laughing?

ROSS: You're gonna.

COLIN: I'm not. What's wrong with being an astronaut?

ROSS: Nothing! It's awesome and amazing and exciting! It's like the best job in the whole world!

COLIN: Well, then, there you go. I don't see the problem.

ROSS: It's hard to get in.

COLIN: What do you have to do?

ROSS: First, you have become a pilot in the Air Force by going through the Air Force Academy. Then you have to apply to the space program and be selected as one of the best pilots. Then there's astronaut training and all sorts of other cool shit like that before they let you go up.

COLIN: Wow.

ROSS: My dad says there's no way I could ever do it.

COLIN: Your dad said that?

ROSS: (*nodding*) He says that becoming an astronaut is harder than getting struck by lightning and winning the lottery on the same day.

COLIN: Well, it does seem pretty hard. I mean, how many people have ever made it?

ROSS: 321.

COLIN: Huh?

ROSS: There have been 321 astronauts since the space program began in 1959.

COLIN: Wow. Nice trivia.

ROSS: I read it in a book.

COLIN: (*in disbelief*) You read a book that wasn't required for school?

ROSS: Yeah. Space books are the best. I read this one book called, "Lost Moon" that Jim Lovell wrote. It's pretty cool.

COLIN: Jim Lovell?

ROSS: Yeah. Apollo 13? Didn't you ever see that Tom Hanks movie?

COLIN: Which one?

ROSS: Apollo 13.

COLIN: Oh. No.

ROSS: I'll have to let you borrow it. It's based on this book. It's really good.

COLIN: Cool.

(*Beat.*)

ROSS: I tell you, being an astronaut would be so cool. You know? And I really wanna do it too.

COLIN: Well, then. I'm behind you 110 percent.

ROSS: Really?

COLIN: Yeah, why not? I'll even try and help you get there.

ROSS: Wow man, thanks.

COLIN: That's what friends are for.

ROSS: Yeah.

(*Beat.*)

COLIN: Now how about you tackle problem number three?

ROSS: Oh yeah. Right.

(*Ross takes up his notebook and goes back to work for a moment then stops.*)

Did I tell you about this super cool test plane they have at NASA?

COLIN: Ross.

ROSS: It's so awesome. It's like this big-ass cargo jet that takes you up really high and then just falls so you can experience weightlessness.

COLIN: Ross.

ROSS: They call it The Vomit Comet.

COLIN: Ross.

ROSS: Yeah?

COLIN: Problem number three.

ROSS: Right, right. (*He returns to his work*)

(*Fade to black.*)

Scene 3

Mid-afternoon three weeks later, ROSS is sitting and trying with much difficulty to light a cigarette. A fishing pole and small tackle box sit beside him.

ROSS: (*with frustration*) Come on. Stupid lighter.

    (*COLIN enters with his pole. ROSS hides the cigarette and the*

    lighter and takes up his pole.)

COLIN: Hey, man. Sorry I'm late.

ROSS: No sweat.

COLIN: (*sitting down next to him and preparing his pole*) My mom

    made me clean my room.

ROSS: Again? Didn't you just do it yesterday?

COLIN: Yeah. I guess it wasn't good enough.

ROSS: Why don't you just tell her off?

COLIN: (*setting his pole down*) Excuse me?

ROSS: Yeah. Tell her that you ain't cleanin' it.

COLIN: I don't think so.

ROSS: Why not?

COLIN: 'Cause she'd kill me, that's why.

ROSS: She wouldn't. She's your mother.

COLIN: (*picking his pole up and preparing to fish*) It's not a big deal.

ROSS: No. Not now. But are you gonna let your mother dictate your every move?

COLIN: (*a little confused*) No.

ROSS: (*casting his line*) Oh no?

COLIN: No.

ROSS: When was the last time you broke the rules?

COLIN: (*casting his line*) I've broken the rules plenty of times.

ROSS: Like when? (*He reels in*)

(*Pause.*)

COLIN: Like the other day.

ROSS: When?

COLIN: Tuesday. Remember?

ROSS: No. Refresh my memory.

(*Colin reels in.*)

COLIN: My mom told me to be back by ten. I didn't get home 'til 10:02.

ROSS: That doesn't count.

COLIN: Sure it does. She was pissed. I wasn't allowed to have a snack before bed like I usually do.

ROSS: (*casting*) What a punishment.

COLIN: Shut up. (*he casts his line*) What kind of things do you do?

ROSS: Lots of stuff.

COLIN: Like what?

ROSS: (*thinking*) Well, uh—

COLIN: See. Nothing.

ROSS: I cut class.

COLIN: You didn't.

ROSS: I did.

COLIN: Liar.

ROSS: I did.

COLIN: When?

ROSS: Yesterday.

COLIN: Which class?

ROSS: English.

COLIN: What? You were skipping?

   (*reeling in and setting his pole down*)

   I thought you went home sick.

ROSS: (*reeling in his line*) Do I look sick?

COLIN: Where were you?

ROSS : Does it matter? I skipped a class, and that's more than I can

   say about you.

COLIN: But where did you go?

ROSS: I'm not gonna tell you my secret hideaway.

COLIN: Come on.

ROSS: I don't think so.

COLIN: Well, what if I wanna skip a class.

ROSS: But you won't.

COLIN: I might.

ROSS: You won't.

COLIN: Why not?

ROSS: You aren't the skipping type.

COLIN: Tell me where you went.

ROSS: (*setting his pole down*) I don't know.

COLIN: You went here didn't you? You went here and fished or

   something.

ROSS: Please.

COLIN: Did you go home?

ROSS: Nope.

COLIN: Where did you go, Ross?

   (*Pause.*)

ROSS: (*slyly*) Over to the fence by the library.

COLIN: The fence by the library? That doesn't sound exciting.

ROSS: Shows how much you know.

COLIN: Why did you go there?

ROSS: This girl Brigid invited me.

COLIN: Brigid, who's Brigid?

ROSS: This girl. I met her in study hall.

COLIN: When? You never told me.

ROSS: It didn't come up.

COLIN: It's coming up now.

ROSS: And I'm telling you.

COLIN: What's she like?

ROSS: Awesome.

COLIN: That's descriptive.

ROSS: She's older.

COLIN: How old?

ROSS: She's seventeen.

COLIN: Seventeen?

ROSS: Yeah. Cool, huh?

COLIN: Is she a senior?

ROSS: No, sophomore.

COLIN: How is she seventeen and a sophomore?

ROSS: She failed a couple times along the way. It happens to the best of us.

COLIN: Failed? How?

ROSS: I don't know. What is this? Twenty questions?

COLIN: Sorry. Just asking.
(*picking up his fishing pole again*)
So, what'd you do at the fence?
(*Ross smirks.*)
What?

ROSS: (*beaming*) Had a cigarette.

COLIN: Ross!

ROSS: What?

COLIN: You smoke?

ROSS: It's not like I'm addicted. I just tried it. She just came up to me during seventh period and was like, "Hey, kid. Come have a cigarette with me."

COLIN: Just like that?

ROSS: Yeah. And I was like, "Now?" And she was like, "Yeah." And I was like, "But we have class." And she was like, "So?" Like she didn't even care!

COLIN: That's probably why she failed so many times.

ROSS: (*ignoring his comment*) So, I went. And I don't care what DARE says, smoking does make you feel cool. 'Cause I did. It was awesome. I met a bunch of her friends there too. They all had piercings and tattoos and shit. (*recalling*) They were so cool.

COLIN: Yeah.

(*he casts his line*)

Real cool.

ROSS: They were! (thinking) I think I might make it a regular thing.

COLIN: Ross!

ROSS: What?

COLIN: I thought you said you were just gonna try it?

ROSS: I did. But I have tried it, and I liked it.

COLIN: Man, I don't know.

ROSS: What?

COLIN: I just don't think it's my scene that's all.

ROSS: (*confused*) Well, it doesn't have to be your scene. I'm the one doing it.

COLIN: (*covering*) No— Right, I know.

ROSS: Besides if I hang out with them during eighth period then I can still come hang out with you after school and fish or something.

COLIN: (*reeling in*) Yeah, yeah. (*testing the water*) And maybe sometimes I can cut and hang out with you guys.

ROSS: Well...

COLIN: Yeah, and then we can all come up here and mess around or something.

ROSS: (*not sure*) Yeah.

(*Ross pulls out his cigarette and tries to light it again.*)

COLIN: You're gonna smoke now?

ROSS: Yeah.

(*stopping*)

Is that okay?

COLIN: Yeah... I guess.

ROSS: Do you wanna try one?

COLIN: I don't know.

ROSS: (*pulling a few loose cigarettes out of his pocket*) I have a couple others.

COLIN: Why don't you save them.

ROSS: It's okay, I can get more from Brigid on Monday.

COLIN: No, really, it's fine.

ROSS: You sure?

COLIN: Yeah.

ROSS: (putting the loose ones away) Okay.

(*Ross continues to try to light the cigarette. Colin sits next to him and breaks off a piece of wood from the bridge. Ross' cigarette lights and he takes a drag. He coughs then smiles. Colin looks at him then throws the piece of wood into the river. Fade to black.*)

Scene 4

Evening in January, ROSS and COLIN are sliding on ice that has formed on the bridge.

COLIN: Check this.

  (*Colin slides, jumps, spins, and lands safely.*)

ROSS: Nice.

COLIN: Nice? Let's see what you got.

ROSS: Okay.

  (*Ross tries to duplicate Colin' stunt but only does half of the spin*

  and almost falls over at the end.)

COLIN: (*sarcastically*) Real good.

ROSS: Just as good as you.

COLIN: Whatever.

ROSS: Shut up.

COLIN: Gonna make me?

ROSS: Yeah.

COLIN: Just try!

ROSS: Watch me.

  (*Ross lunges at Colin. They slide around on the ice chasing each other and laughing.*)

COLIN: Careful! Don't slip!

ROSS: Jerk!

COLIN: Wouldn't want you to bruise!

ROSS: Hey, hold still!

COLIN: Yeah, right!

  (*Ross stops tired. He coughs.*)

  Too much exercise for you?

ROSS: (*coughing*) Just a little winded.

COLIN: Figures.

ROSS: (*aggressive*) What's that supposed to mean?

COLIN: (*surprised*) Nothing.

ROSS: Oh. Sorry.

COLIN: Calm down.

ROSS: (*walking away*) I am.

COLIN: Okay.

  (*Ross pulls out a pack of cigarettes, puts one in his mouth and
  lights it on the first try.*)

  Getting good with that lighter.

ROSS: (*through the cigarette*) Practice.

  (*Ross exhales a large cloud of smoke. Colin stands at a distance.
  After a moment he starts digging into his pockets.*)

COLIN: Oh! I just remembered.

ROSS: What?

COLIN: I picked something up for you.

ROSS: (*going to Colin*) Yeah? What is it?

COLIN: (*still digging*) I'm trying to find it.

  (*He pulls out a stack of papers and sorts through them. He finds a
  brochure.*)

  (*holding it out*) Ha!

ROSS: Found it?

COLIN: Yeah.

ROSS: (*taking a drag*) What is it?

COLIN: (*handing it to him*) Here.

(*Ross takes it and reads the cover.*)

It's about the Air Force Academy. There's stuff in there about admissions and things.

ROSS: (*excited*) Really?

(*He starts paging through it.*)

COLIN: Yeah. There's a list of the physical requirements and stuff about academics.

ROSS: (*reading*) "Many will apply, few will be accepted."

(*he smiles*)

"To become one of them, you'll have to meet the Academy's high admission standards and the fierce competition for appointment. During our selection process, we evaluate you on academic, extracurricular and physical fitness criteria and select candidates with the 'whole-person' potential needed to successfully complete the Academy's educational, military and athletic programs — and serve as Air Force officers." Dude, this is so cool.

COLIN: (*pointing*) Did you see the planes they let you fly?

ROSS: (*turning*) Yeah, yeah. They're like these sailplanes. Aren't they slick?

COLIN: Yeah, and then they have these simulators so that you practice like you're in a real jet.

ROSS: Wow, man. This is awesome.

COLIN: Isn't it though?

ROSS: Thanks. (*looking through the catalogue*) My dad just keeps telling me that I should give it up, but I tell you, I think I can make it.

COLIN: Totally. But—

ROSS: But what?

COLIN: (*pointing at his cigarette*) You might wanna stop doing that sort of thing.

ROSS: What sort of thing?

COLIN: Smoking.

ROSS: (*taking a drag*) Oh, come on.

COLIN: I'm serious. Did you see those physical requirements?

ROSS: I know the physical requirements.

(*Colin takes the brochure and finds the requirements.*)

COLIN: (*reading*) Seven pull-ups.

ROSS: I can do that.

COLIN: (*reading*) Fifty-eight sit-ups

ROSS: Cake.

COLIN: (*reading*) Thirty-five push-ups

ROSS: Colin, I know the requirements. I can do all that. Smoking won't stop me from doing that.

COLIN: Oh yeah? How about the running?

ROSS: Running?

COLIN: Yeah. (*reading*) One and a half miles in twelve minutes and twenty five seconds.

ROSS: (*a little worried*) Twelve minutes isn't so hard.

COLIN: Ross, I've never even seen you run a mile.

ROSS: I can run a mile, thank you very much. What kind of man can't run a mile?

COLIN: You.

ROSS: Screw you, Colin

(*He takes another drag of his cigarette and then throws it into the river. He goes for another.*)

COLIN: Another, eh? Looks like you're getting addicted.

ROSS: (*aggravated*) Lay off, okay?

COLIN: Sorry. Just trying to be a friend.

ROSS: (*snapping*) Well, you can stop.

(*He starts to light his new cigarette*)

COLIN: What?

ROSS: (*apologetic*) I didn't mean that.

COLIN: No?

ROSS: No. I didn't.

COLIN: Okay.

   (*Silence.*)

   (*Ross finishes lighting and takes a long drag.*)

   Look, I gotta go study.

ROSS: I thought we were gonna study together?

COLIN: My mom needs me at home. She doesn't like me staying out so late.

ROSS: Come on, Colin.

COLIN: No, really. I have to go.

ROSS: Colin.

COLIN: I have to go. I'll see you tomorrow at school.

ROSS: Okay. See ya.

   (*Colin starts to go.*)

   (*calling after him*) Hey, Col.

COLIN: Yeah?

ROSS: Thanks for the brochure.

COLIN: Don't mention it.

   (*Colin exits.*)

ROSS: Bye.

   (*Ross looks through the brochure, takes a drag on the cigarette, then stops. He looks at the cigarette then at the brochure. He goes to throw the cigarette in the river, but stops. He takes another puff. Fade to black.*)

Scene 5

Just after midnight two weeks later, ROSS is standing smoking a cigarette. Ross looks around and then takes a long drag on the cigarette.

BRIGID (*O.S.*): Ross?

ROSS: Brigid?

BRIGID (O.S.): Where are you?

ROSS: I'm out here.

   (*BRIGID enters.*)

BRIGID: Man, this place is hard to find.

ROSS: Did you get lost?

BRIGID: Only twice.

ROSS: (*smirking*) Good.

BRIGID: (*looking around*) This is a slick bridge.

ROSS: Yeah? (*taking a drag on his cigarette*) It's okay.

BRIGID: (*turning toward him*) Too modest.

ROSS: So, what'd you wanna come out here for?

BRIGID: I wanted to see where you were always going. I figured it
   might be a happening place.

ROSS: Please.

BRIGID: No, seriously. I wanted to check out its appeal firsthand.

(*gesturing around*) It is nice.

ROSS: Thanks.

BRIGID: Besides. I figured it was time we had some alone time.

ROSS: Alone time?

BRIGID: (*moving closer to him*) Yeah, you know...

(*She takes his cigarette, smokes it and exhales in his face.*)

Alone time.

ROSS: (*smiling*) Right.

BRIGID: (*looking at the cigarette*) Upgraded to the reds?

ROSS: Yeah. You said they were better.

BRIGID: You skeptical or something?

ROSS: No, no. They are better.

BRIGID: Good.

(*She hands him back the cigarette.*)

I brought us a little ice breaker.

(*She reaches into her pocket and pulls out a flask.*)

ROSS: (*taking a puff*) What's that?

BRIGID: Diet soda.

ROSS: Really?

BRIGID: No, dumb ass. It's whiskey. I swiped it from my dad's liquor
cabinet. The drunken idiot never thinks to lock it.

ROSS: Whiskey?

BRIGID: What? Did I stutter?

ROSS: No. I've— I've just never had it before.

BRIGID: (*smiles*) First time for everything.

ROSS: I don't know.

BRIGID: Come on, Ross.

(*She unscrews the top and wafts the flask under his nose. He
backs away at the smell. She laughs and takes a drink.*)

Ah. Now that hits the spot. (*holding it out*) Now you get over here and take some.

ROSS: I don't really want to.

BRIGID: Ross, don't be a loser.

ROSS: I'm not. I just want to finish my cigarette first.

BRIGID: You can do both.

ROSS: I don't want the tastes to mix.

(*Brigid takes his cigarette, has a long drag that reduces the rest of it to ash. Then flicks it into the river. She holds out the flask again.*)

BRIGID: Bottoms up.

ROSS: (*taking it*) You owe me a cigarette.

BRIGID: Sure.

(*Ross looks at the flask with apprehension.*)

Come on, man.

(*He takes a quick swig and almost chokes.*)

Exhale, man. Exhale!

ROSS: (*coughing*) I am exhaling!

BRIGID: (*laughing*) Good stuff, huh? Dad's favorite. He saves it for special occasions. He won't notice that it's missing until Easter. Besides he's becoming more of a bar man these days.

ROSS: Your family drinks whiskey on Easter?

BRIGID: We're Jewish.

ROSS: (*not getting it*) Oh.

(*Pause. Brigid has another drink.*)

You know, my dad would kill me if he caught me doing this.

BRIGID: Don't worry, he's not gonna catch you.

ROSS: I'm supposed to start work at his store tomorrow morning.

BRIGID: He's not gonna catch you.

ROSS: I hope not.

BRIGID: You worry too much.

ROSS: I gotta lot to worry about.

BRIGID: (*handing him the flask*) Mellow out.

ROSS: (*taking it*) It's just that my dad's been ragging on me all the time lately.

BRIGID: Drink.

(*He drinks and hands the flask back.*)

ROSS: I don't know what it's all about, you know? He says I'm not living up to my potential. That I have all these high hopes but no will to accomplish them.

BRIGID: (*taking a drink*) What high hopes are these?

ROSS: You'll laugh.

BRIGID: Try me.

ROSS: I'm serious, you'll laugh.

BRIGID: Do you need another drink first?

ROSS: Maybe.

BRIGID: (*handing him the flask*) Good answer.

(*He takes a drink.*)

How you feelin', kiddo?

ROSS: Good... Yeah. Real good.

BRIGID: Nice.

(*She gets out her cigarettes and lights one.*)

So, these high hopes?

ROSS: Don't laugh.

BRIGID: I won't. Jesus. You sound like a broken record.

ROSS: Okay, fine. I wanna go to the Air Force Academy... become an astronaut.

BRIGID: An astronaut?

ROSS: Yeah.

(*She busts out laughing.*)

I said, don't!

BRIGID: I can't help it. I mean— Man. An astronaut. Now that is something.

(*She takes a drink.*)

ROSS: You don't think I can do it?

BRIGID: Kiddo, I think you can do what ever you want.

ROSS: Thank you.

BRIGID: But astronaut... That's a hard **gig**.

ROSS: That's what my dad keeps saying.

BRIGID: Maybe it's true.

ROSS: I mean it is. Don't get me wrong. (*sincere*) But I can do it. I
    can.

BRIGID: Why though?

ROSS: 'Cause it's my dream.

BRIGID: But what if you don't make it? Then where will you be?

ROSS: I don't know. I guess I'll be stuck at my dad's store.

BRIGID: Ah! Now there's an aspiration.

ROSS: What? Working for my dad?

BRIGID: Yeah!

ROSS: Why?

BRIGID: Look. Tell me, honestly, is your dad ever gonna fire you?

ROSS: I don't know.

BRIGID: No. He's not.

ROSS: He's not?

BRIGID: No! You're his son! He's required to keep you around!

ROSS: I guess.

BRIGID: Think of how sweet a gig that is!

ROSS: Working for my dad?

BRIGID: Yeah. You can do whatever the fuck you want and you won't
    get fired.

ROSS: I don't know.

BRIGID: Come on, don't be dense. You got a sweet deal. You can skip
    work, sleep on the job, whatever. After awhile you'll still inherit

the store, and then you'll be set for life! You're his son, man!

ROSS: I guess so.

BRIGID: Don't guess. Know!

ROSS: Okay. (*thinking*) But how is that better than being an astronaut.

BRIGID: (*pounding him on the head*) Hello! Is anybody in there?

ROSS: Hey! Watch it!

BRIGID: If you join the Army—

ROSS: Air Force.

BRIGID: Whatever.

(*she takes a drink*)

If you do that, then you gotta work like nonstop from now till eternity.

ROSS: So?

BRIGID: You don't wanna do that, do you?

ROSS: I thought I did.

BRIGID: Believe me, you don't.

ROSS: (*not convinced*) Okay.

BRIGID: But if you work for your dad, you can slack off indefinitely!

(*taking a drag*) Not to mention the perks.

ROSS: Perks?

BRIGID: Do I have to spell everything out for you?

ROSS: No. I get you.

(*Pause. She takes a drink and hands the flask to Ross. He takes it and looks at it.*)

Okay, no, I don't get you. What perks?

BRIGID: You're killing me, kid.

ROSS: What? I don't get it.

(*She puts her arm around him and takes a drag close to his ear*)

BRIGID: Free stuff.

ROSS: Free stuff?

BRIGID: Yeah.

ROSS: I don't get free stuff.

BRIGID: Sure you do.

ROSS: No, I don't. I get a discount. Ten percent.

BRIGID: No, man. I mean you can take stuff.

ROSS: (unsure) You mean steal it?

BRIGID: (nodding) Yes.

ROSS: I can't steal from my dad's store.

BRIGID: Why not?

ROSS: Because it's my dad's store.

BRIGID: So?

ROSS: Because he'd kill me, and then have me arrested, and then, when I got home, he'd kill me again.

BRIGID: No way.

ROSS: You don't know my dad.

BRIGID: What does that have to do with it?

ROSS: Everything.

BRIGID: You're just scared.

ROSS: Uh, yeah.

BRIGID: Come on, Ross. Don't be a wimp.

ROSS: I'm not.

BRIGID: You are.

ROSS: (adamant) I'm not.

BRIGID: Ross, everyone steals stuff.

ROSS: Maybe, but I don't.

BRIGID: Oh? You don't?

ROSS: I don't.

BRIGID: (screwing the top back on the flask and putting it away) Well, then. I must have mistaken you for someone else.

ROSS: What?

BRIGID: (leaving) I thought you were a cool kid, but I guess I was wrong.

ROSS: Where you going?

BRIGID: I'm not about to date a loser.

ROSS: Date?

BRIGID: Yeah. Date. I liked you. I thought you were cool. But now, I
   guess not.

ROSS: Wait! Wait a second. You liked me?

BRIGID: Yeah.

ROSS: (*almost stammering*) You were gonna date me?

BRIGID: (*going again*) I was. But oh well.

ROSS: No. Wait! Stay.

BRIGID: Why?

ROSS: Because.

BRIGID: Because why?

ROSS: Because I want you to.

BRIGID: I don't know. That's not so much of an argument.

ROSS: I won't be a loser.

BRIGID: No?

ROSS: I'll show you.

BRIGID: Yeah?

ROSS: Give me that flask.

   (*She does so. He unscrews the cap and finishes it.*)

BRIGID: Wow.

   (*He screws the top on and gives it back. He coughs.*)
   You okay?

ROSS: I'm fine. (*taking her hand*) Come on. I know where we can get
   some more.
   You mean...?

ROSS: Yeah. I have a discount.

   (*He starts to go. She hangs on to his hand, pulls him close and
   kisses him.*)

(*smiling*) Nice.

BRIGID: (*putting an arm around him*) Let's go, Kiddo.

(*They exit. Fade to Black.*)

Scene 6

Late afternoon two weeks later COLIN and ROSS are studying. They are sharing Colin's text book. Colin turns the page.

ROSS: (*stopping him*) No, no, not yet.

COLIN: We've been on this page for like five minutes.

ROSS: I'm not done yet.

COLIN: Are you close?

ROSS: Yeah. Hold on... hold on... okay... good. Turn the page.

COLIN: (*turning the page*) Finally. You read slower than a turtle in a bowl of molasses.

ROSS: What?

COLIN: Nevermind. Just keep reading. We still have the problems to do.

ROSS: Don't get snappy with me.

COLIN: I'm not. I just want to finish before it gets dark.

ROSS: (*pushing the book towards Colin*) Fine. Then read by yourself. (*Ross gets up and walks away*)

COLIN: Ross.

ROSS: (*not turning around*) Read, Colin.

COLIN: Ross, I said I would share and I will. (an afterthought) I want to.

ROSS: You need to take sharing lessons then. (*turning*) It's not my fault I lost my bookbag. I lost all of my stuff, man. My books, my homework, my folders, a whole pack of reds.

COLIN: (*sarcastic*) Oh dear, how sad.

ROSS: Would you stop ragging on me about smoking! I'm sick of it!

COLIN: Ross, it's illegal, you're only fifteen!

ROSS: So? Lots of fifteen-year-olds smoke.

COLIN: Who?

ROSS: Brigid smoked when she was fifteen.

COLIN: And she's who you should be modeling your life after.

ROSS: What are you trying to say?

COLIN: I'm not trying to say anything.

ROSS: Then what are you saying? Huh?

COLIN: I'm saying that if you want to get in the Air Force Academy like you say all the time maybe you should work at it.

ROSS: (*defensive*) I am working at it.

COLIN: What did you get on that Bio test last week?

ROSS: That was a fluke.

COLIN: What'd you get?

ROSS: "C" minus.

COLIN: "C" minus!

ROSS: Shut up.

COLIN: What about that Algebra test?

ROSS: I'm not doing this.

COLIN: What did you get Ross?

ROSS: A "D" alright?

COLIN: I believe on both of those occasions you blew off our study session.

ROSS: Come on, Colin.

COLIN: Didn't you?

ROSS: Yeah. So what? Life's not all about books.

COLIN: I never said it was. But, then again, I'm not trying to get into the Air Force Academy.

ROSS: So, what is this about? You think I can't make it?

COLIN: It's not about that.

ROSS: Then what?

COLIN: It's not even really about the fucking Air Force Academy.

ROSS: Then what's it about, Colin? Huh? What's it about?
   (*Silence.*)

COLIN: (*he starts to pick up his things*) I'm going home.

ROSS: (*swiping Colin's book*) No.

COLIN: Hey!

ROSS: (*grabbing Colin's shoulder*) What's it about?

COLIN: I don't wanna talk about it.

ROSS: Yes, you do.

COLIN: No, I don't, now let go of me.

ROSS: Colin.

COLIN: (*mimicking*) Ross.

ROSS: What? What is this about? Are you gonna talk to me or what? I thought we talked? I thought that's what friends did.

COLIN: Oh, so we're friends?

ROSS: Yeah. We've always been friends.

COLIN: Funny. I hadn't noticed.

ROSS: What does that mean?

COLIN: Ross, I hardly ever see you anymore. You're caught up with that Brigid girl all the time. Smoking. Doing God-knows-what-else. I don't even know who you are anymore.

ROSS: You don't know who I am?

COLIN: No. What did you do with my best friend?

ROSS: I am your best friend.

COLIN: No, you aren't.

ROSS: How?

COLIN: Best friends are always there for each other. Where have you been these past months?

ROSS: I've been here.

COLIN: You haven't. You've been everywhere else.

(*Silence.*)

Look, man. I don't wanna talk about it. But you really need to start studying if you wanna have a prayer at your dreams.

(*Colin gathers his things*)

ROSS: Where are you going?

COLIN: Home. It's cold out here.

ROSS: You used to like studying in the cold. You said it kept you awake.

COLIN: I changed my mind.

ROSS: Colin, I can't do this by myself.

COLIN: Why? 'Cause I have the only textbook between us?

ROSS: No. (*reconsidering*) Well, yes. That's a part of it. But I want your help.

COLIN: I don't know, man.

ROSS: What you mean, you don't know? You are my friend still, right?

(*No answer*)

Right?

COLIN: Yeah. Of course.

(*Pause.*)

ROSS: Look. I'm sorry if I haven't been around. I'm just tryin' to fit in, you know? You're still my number one friend. My right hand man. My compadre con queso.

COLIN: That doesn't make sense.

ROSS: Like I speak French.

COLIN: It's Spanish.

ROSS: Whatever. Come on, what do you say? Will you help me study?

(*Pause.*)

COLIN: (*reluctant*) Okay. I'll help.

ROSS: Awesome. Let's get to work!

COLIN: Not now though. (*weakly*) Tomorrow.

ROSS: Tomorrow?

COLIN: Same time. (*unconvincing*) I— uh... I gotta clean my room.

ROSS: Didn't you just do that last week?

COLIN: Yeah, uh. You know my mom.

ROSS: Right.

COLIN: Same time tomorrow?

ROSS: Yeah. I'll be there. On the dot.

COLIN: Promise?

ROSS: Promise.

COLIN: (*going*) Alright.

ROSS: See ya.

COLIN: (*turning back*) Bye, Ross.

(*Colin exits. Ross watches him go then pulls out a cigarette and looks at it. Pause. He lights it and takes a drag. Fade to Black.*)

Scene 7

The next night, COLIN sits on the bridge with his backpack next to him throwing sticks into the river. He checks his watch and then gathers his things to go. There is a noise off stage. ROSS and BRIGID enter with shopping bags, mildly drunk.

ROSS: (*seeing Colin*) Aw, shit.

   (*Colin starts to go.*)

   (*stumbling after him*) No, no. Colin! No, don't go! Colin!

   (*Ross grabs Colin by the shoulder.*)

COLIN: Let go of me.

ROSS: Colin. I'm sorry.

COLIN: You're sorry?

ROSS: (*drunk*) I so am.

COLIN: You're two hours late! (*smelling his breath*) And you smell

   disgusting. You drink now, too?

ROSS: A little.

COLIN: Ross, you're only fifteen!

ROSS: (*pointing at Brigid*) So, Brigid's eighteen!

COLIN: (*crossing to Brigid*) So, this is Brigid?

BRIGID: Yeah. Who are you?

COLIN: (*to Ross*) You never even mentioned me?

ROSS: It didn't come up.

COLIN: (*to Brigid*) I'm his best friend. (*to Ross*) Was his best friend.

ROSS: Oh come on, Col. I said I was sorry.

COLIN: (*going to the bags*) And what's all this stuff?

(*He opens one of them an pulls out a bottle of Whiskey. Another has a bottle of Vodka.*)

Ross? Where did you get all of this?

ROSS: (*rushing to the bags*) That's none of your business.

COLIN: (*hanging on to the Whiskey and reading the price sticker*)

This is from your dad's store!

ROSS: (*taking the Whiskey back*) So?

COLIN: Did you steal this?

ROSS: It's my dad's.

COLIN: You stole this!

ROSS: It's my dad's. It's not stealing.

COLIN: (*to Brigid*) Did you make him do this?

BRIGID: Again, who are you?

COLIN: (*shouting*) I'm Colin! Colin!

ROSS: Colin, look. I'm sorry I missed our studying.

COLIN: No, you're not.

ROSS: I am.

COLIN: You're not! All you are is drunk.

ROSS: No!

COLIN: What happened to you?

ROSS: Life. Life happened to me, Colin.

COLIN: Excuse me?

ROSS: I stopped living in the safe world with you. I got out. I saw new places. (*gesturing to Brigid*) I got a girlfriend. A girlfriend, Colin. How about that?

COLIN: (*he turns to go*) I'm going home.

ROSS: Why, Colin? Why do you always go home? What are you so afraid of?

COLIN: (*snapping*) Right now, I'm afraid of you.

ROSS: Why? Because I lived a little? Because I decided not to spend my whole life walled up inside a glass house? (crossing to Colin) Look at you on your judgment seat. What have you ever done? Huh? Colin?

(*Colin looks down.*)

(*Pause.*)

That's right. Nothing. You run away. You always run away.

BRIGID: (*pulling Ross back*) Ross, Come on.

COLIN: What else should I do? Huh? (beat) Who are you, Ross? Who the fuck are you? You're not my best friend, that's for sure. You sold me up the river for some booze and a cheap date. My best friend wouldn't do that. (beat) My best friend's dead, and I don't know who you are.

(*He turns to go.*)

ROSS: (*calling after him*) Things change, buddy. You gotta change with 'em or get left behind.

(*Colin stops and turns. Ross opens the bottle of Whiskey he has been holding and holds it out for Colin to drink. Colin looks at it, then at Ross, then at Brigid. He shakes his head and walks off. Fade to Black.*)

END OF ACT ONE.

ACT TWO

Scene 1

A summer afternoon two years later, COLIN sits fishing. He has a tackle box and a lunch pail next to him. He is singing a popular song loudly and off-key. KATY enters listening. She snickers. Colin continues singing. Her laugh grows. He hears her and stops. He turns around.

Katy: (*through laughter*) If you wanna catch something, you should probably be a little quieter.

COLIN: Huh?

KATY: Of course, I'm not a fisherman. For all I know it might be a new technique.

COLIN: What are you talking about?

KATY: Your singing. As pretty as it was, it might be counterproductive.

COLIN: Oh, that.

KATY: (*with a smile*) Yeah, that.

(*Colin goes back to fishing. Silence. Katy walks across the bridge watching Colin out of the corner of her eye. Colin sees her. He reels in.*)

COLIN: What?

KATY: I didn't say anything.

COLIN: You were looking at me. Is my hair sticking up or something?

KATY: (*joking*) A little.

COLIN: (*concerned*) Really? (*trying to fix it*) Where? Here?

KATY: I was just kidding.

COLIN: (*embarrassed*) Oh.

   (*He sets his pole down.*)

   (*Pause.*)

KATY: (simultaneously with Colin) So, what—?

COLIN: (simultaneously with Katy) So, who—?

   (*Pause.*)

KATY: Sorry.

COLIN: You go.

KATY: No, you. I interrupted you.

COLIN: No, no. You.

   (*Pause.*)

KATY: What's your name?

COLIN: Colin.

KATY: Hi, Colin.

COLIN: (*nervous*) Hi.

   (*He smiles. She smiles. Pause.*)

KATY: (*with a smirk*) I'm Katy.

COLIN: What's so funny?

KATY: Nothing.

   (*Pause.*)

   How are the fish biting?

COLIN: Fish?

KATY: Yeah. (*pointing at the river*) Fish.

COLIN: Oh. I don't know. I haven't caught anything since I was
   twelve.

KATY: So, I guess not good?

COLIN: No. Not so much. (*justifying*) It's relaxing though.

KATY: Oh, so do you lead a stressful life?

COLIN: (*confused*) No.

KATY: Oh.

(Pause.)

So.

COLIN: Yeah?

KATY: (*she smirks*) You fish here a lot?

COLIN: Seriously, what's so funny?

KATY: Nothing's funny.

COLIN: You smile an awful lot.

KATY: Is that bad?

COLIN: I don't know. My mom says anything in excess is bad.

KATY: Do you think I excessively smile?

COLIN: (*daring*) Yes.

KATY: Oh. I was unaware. How about this: (*with an exaggerated pout*) You fish here a lot?

COLIN: (*he smiles*) Better.

KATY: Thank you.

(*Pause.*)

Well?

COLIN: Well what?

KATY: Do you?

COLIN: Do I what?

KATY: Fish here a lot?

COLIN: Oh. Sort of.

KATY: Sort of?

COLIN: Yeah.

KATY: How do you sort of fish here a lot?

COLIN: Well, I meant—

KATY: Yes?

COLIN: I meant I do.

KATY: Oh.

(*Long silence. Katy sits next Colin. Colin watches her suspiciously. Pause.*)

COLIN: Am I supposed to remember you from somewhere?

KATY: No. I don't think so.

COLIN: You sure?

KATY: Yeah. Pretty sure. I don't know you from anywhere.

COLIN: Oh. Okay.

(*Pause.*)

KATY: Why?

COLIN: I was just wondering. Because I didn't either. And I wanted to know if I should have.

KATY: (*sarcastically*) Oh yeah. You don't remember? I'm that girl you dated last summer. By the way, I'm pregnant.

COLIN: (*freaking out*) What?!? I didn't—

KATY: A joke?

COLIN: Oh. Cool. Good one.

(*Silence.*)

So.

KATY: Yeah?

COLIN: You from around here?

KATY: Not really. I mean, I am now, I guess.

COLIN: Oh, so you moved here?

KATY: Well, my parents did. I decided to come along.

COLIN: (*genuine*) You had a choice?

KATY: (*smirking*) Another joke.

COLIN: Oh.

(*Pause.*)

KATY: We move a lot. (*more to herself*) This one was particularly annoying.

COLIN: Why?

KATY: Well, We'd been living just outside of New York for the last two years, you know "the city."

COLIN: Right, yeah.

KATY: And I was all set to graduate from the high school I was going to. I had friends, a boyfriend, a life. Then this summer, my dad was like, "Okay, Katy, we're moving." (*gesturing around*) And here we are. (*pointedly*) To think. In one more year, I would've been on my own.

COLIN : You have a boyfriend?

KATY: (*laughing*) It's funny the things that catch people's ears.

COLIN: What?

KATY: Nevermind. I just found it funny.

COLIN: Found what funny?

KATY: Nevermind.

(*Pause.*)

And no, we broke up when I moved. He was a prick anyway. (*to herself*) Good kisser though. (*to Colin*) Are you a good kisser?

COLIN: (*caught off-guard*) Huh?

KATY: Just kidding. Good reaction though.

(*Silence.*)

Favorite color.

COLIN: What?

KATY: What's your favorite color?

COLIN: (*thinking hard*) Um...

KATY: It's not a trick question.

COLIN: (*defensive*) I know.

KATY: (*backing off*) Okay.

(*Pause.*)

COLIN: Blue.

KATY: Blue?

COLIN: Yeah, what's wrong with blue?

KATY: Nothing.

   (*Pause.*)

   It's just—

COLIN: What?

KATY: Nothing.

COLIN: What?

KATY: It's just plain, that's all. Everyone likes blue.

COLIN: So?

KATY: Why don't you pick a color that's really out there? Like...
   um... hot pink?

COLIN: Because I don't like hot pink.

KATY: I said like hot pink. It doesn't have to be hot pink.

COLIN: But I like blue.

KATY: Okay, okay. Blue it is.

   (*Silence.*)

COLIN: What's your favorite color?

KATY: You can't ask the same question.

COLIN: Why not?

KATY: It's against the rules.

COLIN: What rules?

KATY: The rules of the game.

COLIN: What game?

KATY: The question game.

COLIN: I didn't know we were playing a game.

KATY: So?

COLIN: Then how could I—? How—? But—? (*sighing*) Nevermind.

   (*Katy laughs.*)

   You know, you could stop antagonizing me any time.

KATY: But then what else would I do all day?

COLIN: Hardy-Har-Har.

KATY: Serious? "Hardy-Har-Har?"

COLIN: What's wrong with that?

KATY: No one says that.

COLIN: I do.

KATY: But no one else does.

COLIN: So?

KATY: Ah, you're a rebel.

COLIN: No.

KATY: No, I think you are. Sneering in the face of conformity.

COLIN: What?

   (*Pause.*)

KATY: Say, you wanna go get something to eat?

COLIN: I'm fishing.

KATY: Well, if you haven't caught anything in six years, I think you
   could spare a couple hours.

COLIN: Today might be my lucky day.

KATY: Come have lunch with me.

COLIN: (*holding up his lunch pail*) I packed lunch.

KATY: What is it?

COLIN: (*opening the pail*) Um...

KATY: You don't remember what you packed?

COLIN: (*looking up*) Well...

KATY: Did your mom pack that for you?

COLIN: (*looking back down*) Um...

KATY: (*laughing*) She did! Ha! What'd she make?

COLIN: (*under his breath*) Cucumber sandwiches.

KATY: What?

COLIN: (*out loud*) Cucumber sandwiches.

KATY: Ew. You like that?

COLIN: Not really.

KATY: Then, how about you ditch 'em, and we get you a hamburger.
   My treat.

COLIN: I don't know.

KATY: Just dump it in the river, she won't know.

(*He looks inside the pail, then to Katy who is edging him on. He dumps the contents into the river. Katy smiles. Fade to black.*)

Scene 2

Late night three weeks later. ROSS and BRIGID are sitting on the bridge drinking beer. They each have a six pack that they are both half-way through. They are spitting into the river.

ROSS: (*spitting*) You ever wonder how tall this bridge is?

BRIGID: (*spitting also*) No.

ROSS: (*elbowing Brigid*) Screw you.

BRIGID: (*smiling*) You watch it. I could take you.

ROSS: Please.

BRIGID: (*"fighting words"*) You wanna go?

ROSS: (*taking a drink*) I don't wanna hurt you.

BRIGID: Like that would happen.

ROSS: Yeah, you just stay cocky. I'll get you when you least expect it.

BRIGID: Ooo. I'm scared.

   (*Brigid finishes her beer and drops it into the river. She pulls out a cigarette and lights it. Ross spits*)

ROSS: Colin said it was a twenty foot drop.

BRIGID: (*taking a drag*) Why don't you jump and find out.

ROSS: You first.

BRIGID: I ain't jumpin'. I still have two more beers to drink. Can't let that shit go to waste.

ROSS: Well, I got three.

BRIGID: (*taking another drag*) Falling behind, slacker.

ROSS: Whatever, Jerk.

BRIGID: (*blows smoke at him*) I know. I'm such a jerk.

(*Ross smiles and reaches for another beer. He opens it and takes a drink. Brigid takes another drag.*)

(*Pause.*)

So, how'd you do on that physics test that you were so worried about?

ROSS: Failed it.

BRIGID: Ross.

ROSS: What? I don't know that shit.

BRIGID: I thought you said that you really needed that test.

ROSS: I did. But I failed.

BRIGID: So, now what?

ROSS: I'm fucked, I guess.

BRIGID: You can still pass, it's early in the year.

ROSS: Whatever. School sucks.

BRIGID: I thought you liked school.

ROSS: No. I don't.

BRIGID: Oh.

ROSS: You gotta do what you gotta do, though, right?

BRIGID: Right.

(*Silence.*)

You know, I'm thinking about blowin' it off.

ROSS: School?

BRIGID: Yeah.

ROSS : When? Tomorrow?

BRIGID : No—

ROSS: How 'bout Friday? We can cut and then take a ride up to Ben's cabin. Bet he's still got some of that good stuff left in the sock drawer. (*smiling*) We can smoke up. (*putting an arm around her*) Relax. (*drawing closer*) Have a good time.

BRIGID: (*smirking*) How romantic.

ROSS: I know. I am Mr. Romance.

BRIGID: You sure are.

   (*She takes a drag. He takes a drink.*)

   (*Pause.*)

   But I wasn't talking about this week.

ROSS: No? Why wait?

BRIGID: I'm talking about a more permanent holiday.

ROSS: Permanent?

BRIGID: Yeah. Like droppin' out for good.

ROSS: Droppin' out?

BRIGID: (*taking a drag*) Yeah.

   (*He takes a drink.*)

ROSS: Man. You serious?

BRIGID: Well, what's the point? Huh? I'm a twenty-year-old high school senior. I think my ship has sailed.

ROSS: You only got one more year.

BRIGID: If I pass.

ROSS: You'll pass. This year's the easy one.

BRIGID: Says you. I ain't got brains.

ROSS: And I do?

BRIGID: You're better off than me.

ROSS: Screw that. You're plenty smart.

BRIGID: (*taking another drag*) Whatever.

ROSS: So, you're just gonna give up then?

BRIGID: Well, it ain't givin' up. I've been going to school my whole fucking life. I'm just done with it. I'm ready to do something real.

ROSS: (*taking a drink*) Like what?

(*She shrugs, finishes her cigarette and flicks it into the river.*)

BRIGID: I don't know. I just wanna get outta here.

ROSS: (*drinks again*) And go where?

BRIGID: Geez. What's with all the questions? I haven't got it all figured out yet.

ROSS: Sorry.

(*Silence. He takes another drink. She gets a beer of her own, opens it, and drinks. Pause.*)

I just wanted to know 'cause—

(*Pause.*)

BRIGID: 'Cause why?

ROSS: Maybe I could go too.

BRIGID: (*sighing*) Ross.

ROSS: No, I'm serious. I can drop out too. We can go together.

BRIGID: You just got through telling me how bad of an idea you thought it was.

ROSS: I know.

BRIGID: So, why would you want to come?

ROSS: Well, what else am I going to do?

BRIGID: Um... stay here? Go to school? You gotta do what you gotta do, right?

ROSS: I dunno. Why?

BRIGID: Because you can finish.

ROSS : So can you.

BRIGID: I can't.

ROSS: Neither can I.

(*Ross takes a drink.*)

(*Pause.*)

BRIGID: I thought you wanted to go to college or something.

ROSS: No.

BRIGID: Yes, you did. You used to want to go to that Academy thing.

ROSS: Oh. Air Force Academy.

BRIGID: Yeah, that.

ROSS: Well, I think I already blew that one.

BRIGID: How come?

ROSS: Well, I'm failing physics, I can't run more than five hundred feet without getting winded, I barely have a 2.0 average.

BRIGID: Is that bad?

ROSS: Yeah.

BRIGID: It's better than what I have.

ROSS: It's still bad. Air Force wants the smart kids. That's not me.

(*Brigid drinks. Ross finishes his and tosses the bottle in the river. Silence.*)

So, where we going?

BRIGID: What?

ROSS: When we drop out. Where are we going?

BRIGID: Ross.

ROSS: Come on.

BRIGID: You're not going.

ROSS: Why not?

BRIGID: 'Cause I don't want you to. You need to stay here.

ROSS: You don't want me to go?

BRIGID: No. I want you to stay here.

ROSS: Why don't you want me to go? I'm your boyfriend.

BRIGID: I know.

ROSS: Are you breaking up with me?

BRIGID: You sound like a girl.

ROSS: You are, aren't you.

BRIGID: No. I'm not. I just think that maybe you should stay in school. So, you don't end up like me, a bum.

ROSS: You aren't a bum. You're the coolest person I know.

BRIGID: Yeah? What makes me so cool?

ROSS: You're independent, you don't care what people think about you. You do what ever you want, and other people just have to deal with that. I wanna be able to be like that.

BRIGID: Like what?

ROSS: Like you.

(*Long Silence. She chugs the rest of her beer and throws it into the river. She pulls out another cigarette and lights it. Pause.*)

BRIGID: So, where do you wanna go?

(*He thinks.*)

ROSS: (*smiling*) What about California?

BRIGID: Why there?

ROSS: Nice weather. It doesn't snow in California. It doesn't get cold.

BRIGID: (*smirking*) Okay. California.

ROSS: Really? We're gonna go?

BRIGID: (*takes another drag*) Yeah. Let's do it.

ROSS: (*smiling*) Thanks.

(*Pause.*)

This means a lot.

BRIGID: I know.

(*Pause.*)

ROSS: I don't know what I would do if you left without me.

BRIGID: Shut up.

ROSS: No. Seriously.

BRIGID: (*stern*) No. Seriously. Shut up.

(*Long Silence.*)

ROSS: When you wanna go?

BRIGID: (*shrugs*) How about two weeks? You can swipe your dad's
    car, and we'll be off.

ROSS: Dad's car? All the way to California?

BRIGID: Yeah.

ROSS: He'd call the cops on us.

BRIGID: Do you wanna do this or what?

ROSS : Can't we just take the bus?

BRIGID: (*taking a drag*) No. I hate buses. They smell like feet. Come
    on. It wouldn't be the first time you "borrowed" the car. We'll be in
    California before he ever notices. Besides, isn't he going to some
    grocer's conference soon?

ROSS: Yeah. Two weeks.

BRIGID: It's perfect. We can load up the car with shit from the store,
    and then be off. We'd have like a two day head start, and he'll
    have no idea where to look for us.
    (*Pause.*)
    Come on.

ROSS : Okay. Dad's car it is.

BRIGID: (*patting him on the back*) That's what I'm talking about.
    (*He smiles. Pause. Ross' cell phone rings. Brigid takes a drag. Ross
    answers his phone*)

ROSS: (*into the phone*) Hello? Hey dad. ... What? ... Nothing. ... I'm
    just out with a friend. ... So? It's not that late. ... What? You never
    told me that? ... That'll be at like six in the morning! ... I can't get
    up for that. I didn't— ... You never— ... Whatever. ... Yeah, yeah.
    ... Okay, I will ... Bye.
    (*He hangs up.*)
    That bastard.

BRIGID: What was it?

ROSS: He's making me work at the store tomorrow. We have a
shipment that I have to help unload. He says I signed up for it, but
I know I didn't.

BRIGID: Don't go.

ROSS: I have to.

BRIGID: What's he gonna do?

ROSS: Be pissed at me.

BRIGID: (*taking a drag*) So? You're leaving town in two weeks, right?

ROSS: Oh, yeah. Right.

BRIGID: Blow that shit off.

ROSS: He'll just drag me out of bed and make me go.

  (*Pause. She looks at him and takes a long drag on her cigarette.*)

BRIGID: You could come stay at my place.

ROSS : I could?

BRIGID: Yeah. Two-to-one says my dad's passed out. Tonight's his
drinking night. He wouldn't even notice.

ROSS: You think?

BRIGID: Definitely.

  (*Ross thinks.*)

ROSS : Okay. (*smiling*) Sounds awesome.

BRIGID: Cool.

  (*She take one last drag and playfully blows the smoke in his face.
He coughs. She smiles and kisses him. Fade to black.*)

Scene 3

Night one week later, KATY runs on to the bridge with a set of car keys in hand. She stops and looks behind her.

KATY: Colin?

　(*No response.*)

　Come on, Colin. You're such a slow poke.

　(*COLIN enters, out of breath.*)

　Man, you need to get in shape.

COLIN: (*barely audible through heavy breathing*) Very funny.

KATY: Huh? What was that?

COLIN: (*still breathing hard*) I said, "very funny."

KATY: (*smiling*) I thought it was.

COLIN: Alright, now give me the car keys back.

KATY: What car keys?

COLIN: Katy.

KATY: I don't have any car keys.

COLIN: Come on, we'll be late.

　(*Katy holds the keys over the edge of the bridge.*)

KATY: (*smiling wider*) Oh, you mean these car keys?

　(*Colin tries for them, but Katy pulls them away from him.*)

COLIN: That's not funny.

KATY: I think it is.

COLIN: It isn't.

KATY: I don't know. We may have to consult the judges.

COLIN: Katy.

KATY: Judges?

COLIN: Come on.

KATY: The judges uphold the ruling on the field. This is funny.

COLIN: Katy, everyone else is probably there already.

KATY: I didn't know that you were such a big fan of Denny's.

COLIN: Well, I guess there's more to me than meets the eye.

KATY: (*poking his belly*) I hope not.

COLIN: Hey! Now, that's not funny.

KATY: (*smiling*) You're right. I'm sorry.

COLIN: Good.

KATY: How could I ever make it up to you?

COLIN: You could give me the keys.

KATY: Um... nope.

COLIN: Come on.

KATY: Sorry.

COLIN: Katy, I'm serious. Everyone will be done by the time we get there.

KATY: What's the hurry?

COLIN: I'm not in a hurry.

KATY: You seem like you're in a hurry.

COLIN: I'm not.

KATY: No?

COLIN: I just really want to go.

KATY: I can see.

COLIN: I don't want to mess this up.

KATY: What?

COLIN: Look, I never get invited anywhere. But now, for some
reason, people have invited somewhere, so I want to go.

KATY: Why?

COLIN: I just want to feel a part of something. Fishing can get
lonely.

KATY: (*smirking*) Even when you're a master, like you?

COLIN: (*shaking his head*) Yes. Even then.

(*Pause.*)

KATY: Wouldn't you rather hang out with me?

COLIN: What?

KATY: Don't you like hanging out with me?

COLIN: I do. Very much.

KATY: Then why do you want to leave?

COLIN: I just— I was excited to get invited somewhere.

KATY: What if I invited you somewhere?

COLIN: (*shrugs*) I don't know.

KATY: Let's see.

COLIN: What?

KATY: Colin, would you like to sit on the bridge with me for a bit?

COLIN: Now you're patronizing me.

KATY: I'm not. I'm being serious. (*pointing to her face*) This is a
serious face.

(*Colin laughs.*)

COLIN: Okay, then. I'd love to.

(*They sit.*)

KATY: So. This is lovely.

COLIN: (*smiling*) It is.

KATY: You come here often?

COLIN: Like that's not a line.

KATY: Hey, I never said I was good at this date stuff.

COLIN: Date?

KATY: Well, I asked you to go somewhere and you agreed. Sounds like a date to me.

COLIN: Well, I think you are missing some qualifiers.

KATY: Like what?

COLIN: Well, for it to be a date you would have to like me.

KATY: I do like you.

COLIN: I mean, like more than a friend like.

KATY: Ooo, more-than-a-friend like. That's pretty different.

COLIN: (*insistent*) It is.

KATY: Well, let's say that I do more-than-a-friend like you. Is this a date then?

COLIN: Well, uh...

KATY: I think that it might be.

COLIN: (*looking down*) It might.

(*Katy smiles. Silence.*)

KATY: So, you wanna go to Denny's now?

COLIN: (*nervously*) Yeah.

KATY: (*holding out the keys*) Here's your keys.

(*Colin tries to take them, but Katy pulls away.*)

COLIN: (sighing) Katy.

KATY: What do I get?

COLIN: Huh?

KATY: What do I get?

COLIN: What do you mean?

(*She leans out her cheek and points. Colin smiles.*)

I don't know.

KATY: Everyone is waiting, Colin. You don't want to disappoint them, do you? They might not invite you again.

(*Colin makes a face. Katy taps her cheek. Colin leans in to kiss it. Katy turns and he kisses her on the lips. Colin is surprised. Katy smiles.*)

COLIN: You did that on purpose!

KATY: (innocent) Yeah, so?

COLIN: Does this mean you—?

KATY: Like you more-that-a-friend like?

COLIN: Yeah.

KATY: (*smirking*) Maybe.

(*Pause.*)

You?

COLIN: Me like you?

KATY: (*correcting*) More-than-a-friend like.

COLIN: Right.

(*Pause.*)

Maybe.

(*They smile. She holds out his keys. He goes to take them. She grabs his hand and pulls him close. They kiss again. Fade to black.*)

Scene 4

A few hours after midnight one week later, ROSS is sitting on the bridge smoking. A large backpack stuffed full sits next to him. He looks at his watch, groans, and takes a puff. BRIGID enters. Ross turns.

ROSS: (standing up and tossing the cigarette) Hey. Where've you
   been? We were supposed to leave two hours ago. Where're your
   bags?

BRIGID: We're not going.

ROSS: What do you mean we're not going? I got my dad's car packed
   full of food. We're set for like a month.

BRIGID: I mean we're not going.

ROSS: Why not?

BRIGID: I don't want to.

ROSS: You did two weeks ago.

BRIGID: So, that was two weeks ago, this is today. Today I don't
   wanna go. Let's go take the groceries back.

ROSS: Take them back?

BRIGID: Yeah.

ROSS: No. You're not getting out of this that easily.

BRIGID: Out of what?

ROSS: Why don't you want to go to California?

BRIGID: I just don't okay. Stop giving me the third degree.

ROSS: I'm gonna give you the fucking third degree if I want to!

BRIGID: Calm down.

ROSS: I'm not calming down until you tell me what's up.

BRIGID: Nothing.

ROSS: Bullshit.

BRIGID: Nothing's up, Ross.

ROSS: Don't play games with me.

BRIGID: I'm not.

ROSS: You wanna break up with me.

BRIGID: Ross.

ROSS: I knew it. What was it? Am I not cool enough?

BRIGID: Come on.

ROSS: Tell me! Tell me, I can fix it!

BRIGID: Christ.

ROSS: What is it? Do I not drink enough for you? Do I cramp your
    style? Or— Or did you find someone else?

BRIGID: Ross, knock it off.

ROSS: It's that Mike guy right?

BRIGID: Mike?

ROSS: Yeah, that guy we met at the concert.

BRIGID: Who? (*remembering*) No!

ROSS: Then who is it, Brigid?

BRIGID: It's nobody.

ROSS: Then why are you doing this to me?

BRIGID: I'm not doing anything to you.

ROSS: You're leaving me.

    (*Pause.*)

BRIGID: Look, it's not you.

ROSS: Are you serious? Are you actually using that line?

BRIGID: It's not a line.

ROSS: Then what the fuck is it?

(*Silence.*)

BRIGID: Look at you. Do you remember your life before you met me?

ROSS: Yeah. I was a loser.

BRIGID: No. You were a bright kid. Might have even had a future.

ROSS: What? Are you taking about the Air Force? Some future that would have been. Working nonstop all day everyday.

BRIGID: Stop it! That's not what you really think.

ROSS: It is.

BRIGID: It's what I told you to think. Everything you do is because I told you to.

ROSS: No, I do things 'cause I want to.

BRIGID: Do you?

ROSS: What are you talking about.

BRIGID: Ross, I fucked you up. You were a nice kid before, but then I came along.

ROSS: You said I was a loser.

BRIGID: I sorta liked that.

ROSS: You did?

BRIGID: Yeah. But now look at you. You're just like me. No future.

ROSS: You have a future.

BRIGID: Yeah? In prison, maybe. Ross, I've messed my life up so much, you wouldn't even know.

ROSS: Brigid. You haven't messed anything up. You're great.

BRIGID: Stop saying shit like that. I'm not. I'm a mess. And I'm turning you into a mess too.

ROSS: Brigid. You're the best thing that ever happened to me.

BRIGID: (*snapping*) Shut up!

(*Pause.*)

ROSS: Look, I didn't do anything that I didn't wanna do. You didn't
   make me do anything.

BRIGID: Yes, I did.

ROSS: No.

BRIGID: Come on. You wouldn't have done shit like that on your own.

ROSS: (*upset*) I would have.

BRIGID: Come on, Ross.

ROSS: No. Don't talk like that. There's nothing wrong with me.
   There's nothing wrong with you. You didn't corrupt me or ruin my
   life or anything.

BRIGID: (*with growing emotion*) What do you know, huh?

ROSS: I know that you're the goddamn love of my life.

BRIGID: Christ! You don't even know what that means!

ROSS: (*hanging on*) I do! And you are. You're wonderful, you hear
   me? You didn't mess up anyone. Your life is fine, my life is fine,
   things are just fine!

BRIGID: They aren't!

ROSS : They are! Now let's get in the car and go to California!

BRIGID: (*getting frustrated*) I'm not going to California!

ROSS: (*yelling*) Yes you are! We are! That's what we're doing!

BRIGID: No.

ROSS: Yes! Brigid, don't you give up on me.

BRIGID: I'm not! Ross, I'm not! I'm not giving up on you for the first
   time ever.

ROSS: What?

BRIGID: I fucked up my life, but I'm not gonna let you fuck up yours!

ROSS: My life isn't fucked up for Christ's sake!

BRIGID: Ross!

ROSS: It's not! My life is just fine! This is the way things are
   supposed to be! You and me together. That's all that's supposed to
   matter. It is! And now we're supposed to go to California!

BRIGID: I'm not going.

ROSS: You are.

BRIGID: I'm not, Ross.

ROSS: Brigid.

BRIGID: You shouldn't either.

ROSS: Come on.

BRIGID: No, Ross.

ROSS: (*picking up his backpack*) Fine. I'll go without you.

BRIGID: Ross. Don't.

ROSS: I'm going.

BRIGID: No.

ROSS: (*yelling*) I am! (attacking) Why are you doing this? You're ruining everything. You're changing everything.

BRIGID: I'm trying to make it right.

ROSS: Well, you aren't. You suck at making it right.

BRIGID: (*hurt*) I'm sorry.

ROSS: I'm going now. Don't you dare call my dad or anything like that.

BRIGID: I won't.

(*She sits. Ross starts to go. He stops and looks back. Silence.*)

ROSS: Brigid.

(*No answer.*)

Brigid?

(*She does not look up.*)

Fine. Goodbye.

(*Ross exits. Brigid looks up and watches him go. She looks back down at the water. Fade to black.*)

Scene 5

Afternoon two weeks later, KATY and COLIN are at the bridge studying.

KATY: (*to her book*) So, I don't get this.

COLIN: What don't you get?

KATY: (*to Colin*) I can do the formulas, but I can't memorize the laws. (*with disdain*) Newton can just go memorize his own fucking laws.

COLIN: But you need the laws to use the formulas.

KATY: Maybe, maybe not.

COLIN: I think you've been studying a little too hard.

KATY: What's the first law again? Object in motion will stay in motion?

COLIN: You forgot the rest of it.

KATY: Yeah, yeah. (*reciting from memory*) An object in motion will stay in motion and an object at rest will stay at rest unless acted upon by an outside force. Is that it?

COLIN: Yup. What about number, uh...

KATY: Don't you dare say three.

COLIN: Three.

KATY : I said, not three.

COLIN: Too bad. Three.

KATY: Jerk.

COLIN: Sorry. Three?

KATY: I'm not answering.

COLIN: You have to.

KATY: Nuh uh.

COLIN: Come on, you know this one.

KATY: I really don't.

COLIN: You know it.

KATY: My mind is blank. What is it?

COLIN: Not telling.

KATY: What?

COLIN: I'm not gonna tell you.

KATY: How come.

COLIN: You have to take a guess.

KATY: You are supposed to be helping me learn this, not playing games.

COLIN: But games are more fun.

KATY: Oh, are they?

COLIN: Yup. They are.

KATY: How do you like this game?

(*Katy jumps on Colin and wrestles around with him. She starts to tickle him and he laughs uncontrollably.*)

COLIN: No! Stop! No, that tickles! Katy!

KATY: (*still tickling*) It's just a game, Colin!

COLIN: (*laughing*) Stop, please!

KATY: Aw, come on.

COLIN: It tickles!

KATY: (*stopping*) Really? I didn't notice.

(*She smiles. He rolls over, pins her down, and starts tickling her.*)

COLIN: Ah ha!

KATY: Hey! That's not fair!

COLIN: I said it was a game, but I never said it was fair.

KATY: Stop! No! Truce! Truce!

COLIN: Okay, truce.

(*He stops they look at each other and smile for a moment. Pause. Katy jumps Colin and tickles him relentlessly. Colin laughs so hard he can barely breathe.*)

KATY: Fooled you!

COLIN: You called a truce!

KATY: Yup!

COLIN: Knock it off!

KATY: Tell me the Third Law of Motion!

COLIN: Never!

KATY: Third Law!

COLIN: You'll never make me talk.

(*She gets to a spot where it really tickles. He laughs really loudly.*)

No! Fine! I'll tell you! I'll tell you!

KATY: Tell me!

COLIN: Every action has an equal and opposite reaction!

KATY: (*stopping*) Thank you.

(*She goes and makes a note in her notebook.*)

COLIN: You are such a cheater.

KATY: You gonna call your mom?

COLIN: No.

KATY: Good. I wouldn't want her to crash our party.

COLIN: Oh yeah?

KATY: (*smiling*) Yup.

(*They laugh. Colin goes back to his reading. Katy watches him for a moment.*)

COLIN: (*catching her*) What?

KATY: (*smirking*) Nothing.

COLIN: Yeah right.

KATY: Can't I just look at you?

COLIN: No.

KATY: Why?

COLIN: It's creepy.

KATY: Why?

COLIN: I don't know.

KATY: (*romantically*) What if I am gazing longingly?

COLIN: What?

KATY: (*less poetic*) What if I'm thinking about jumping your bones?

COLIN: (*embarrassed*) Well— I don't know.

(*She laughs.*)

There you go again. Laughing. Always laughing. People are gonna think you're a loony.

KATY: "A loony?" Who talks like you?

COLIN: I don't know. I do I guess.

KATY: Clever.

COLIN: It was.

(*She smiles.*)

KATY: (*setting her work aside*) Question.

COLIN: Answer.

KATY: What do you want to do after high school?

COLIN: (*caught off-guard*) I don't know. I guess college.

KATY: Where?

COLIN: I was thinking about State.

KATY: Oh.

COLIN: What?

KATY: Nothing.

COLIN: That wasn't a nothing "Oh."

KATY: Well, that's like forty-five minutes away.

COLIN: So?

KATY : I just figured that after eighteen years here, you'd be itching to get out of here.

COLIN: No, not really. I like it here.

KATY: Yeah. But don't you ever wanna travel? Try somewhere else?

COLIN: Like you did?

KATY: Well, for me it wasn't really a choice. But I did enjoy living in different places.

(*Pause.*)

COLIN: Well, I've thought about going places.

KATY: Yeah?

COLIN: Yeah.

KATY: Where?

COLIN: I dunno.

KATY: Come on, Colin.

COLIN: Well...

KATY : Where?

COLIN: I used to really want to go to New York City.

KATY: The city? Really?

COLIN: Yeah.

KATY: It's so awesome there!

COLIN: That's what I thought.

KATY: It's like there's always something going on.

COLIN: Way different then here.

KATY: Yeah. And, oh you'll love this,—

COLIN: What?

KATY: They have... more than one bridge.

(*Colin laughs.*)

COLIN: I don't think you can fish off of those.

KATY: Well. Maybe not.

(*They laugh. Pause.*)

Why don't you apply to a school in New York then?

COLIN: New York?

KATY: Yeah. Why not?

COLIN: I don't know.

KATY: Why?

COLIN: I don't think I could live there.

KATY: Why? It sounds like you'd love it.

COLIN: Yeah. But there's just so many people. And, if you haven't noticed, I have trouble with people.

KATY: Do you have trouble with me?

COLIN: No.

KATY: I'm a person.

COLIN: You know what I mean.

KATY: No. Explain it to me.

(*He shrugs.*)

COLIN: Nevermind.

(*He goes back to studying.*)

KATY: Colin.

COLIN: What?

KATY: Explain it to me.

COLIN: I don't really want to.

KATY: You can't just not talk about things.

COLIN: What?

KATY: Don't be afraid. Say what you're thinking.

COLIN: I'm not afraid.

KATY: You're not?

COLIN: No. I just— I— I just don't wanna talk about it. You know?

KATY: Yeah. I know.

(*Pause.*)

I won't make fun of you, if that's what you're thinking.

COLIN: (*frustrated*) Why are you pushing it?

KATY: I'm not.

COLIN: You are.

KATY: Colin, I just wanna talk.

(*He doesn't answer.*)

What's wrong?

COLIN: Nothing.

KATY: There is.

COLIN: There isn't. Please stop making a big deal about this.

KATY: (*she moves close to him*) I'm not. You are.

(*He turns away.*)

I'm not gonna stop bothering you.

COLIN: (*almost whining*) Why?

KATY: Because that's what you want me to do.

(*Pause.*)

COLIN: (*not serious*) You're such a jerk.

KATY: I know. Tell me what you're afraid of.

(*He looks at her.*)

COLIN: I'm scared of— It's just— I don't know how— I can't talk to people, you know? I'm afraid of what they're thinking. And I just don't know how to interact with them.

(*He looks to her. Katy puts an arm around him.*)

And I... I'm not good at making friends. (looking away) Like you're the only good friend I have right now. And I feel nervous talking to you. It's like anything I say could be the wrong thing and then I would mess this up. And I just can't do that.

(*Beat*)

If I were to go to New York. There would be all these people around judging me. I wouldn't know how to talk to them. I wouldn't be able to make friends.

KATY: Do you remember how we became friends?

COLIN: Yeah. You wouldn't leave me alone.

KATY: Right. But you were able to talk to me. After a while you were really opening up. You even told me your favorite color: hot pink.

COLIN: Blue.

KATY: Are you sure?

COLIN: Yes.

KATY: (*smirking*) I could have sworn you said hot pink.

COLIN: (*starting to smile*) I didn't.

KATY: Well. I guess I'll just have to take your word for it.

COLIN: (*smiling now*) I guess you will.

(*He puts his head on her shoulder*)

(*Long Pause.*)

KATY: How about we both apply to school in New York.

COLIN: (*perking up*) You too?

KATY: Yeah. We'll both do it and then we can go together. I can help you make friends at the beginning and then soon enough you'll be out on your own.

COLIN: You'd do that?

KATY: Colin, I love New York City. I would give anything to be able to move back there.

COLIN: You're really gonna do that?

KATY: Yeah. We'll do it together.

(*He smiles.*)

COLIN: Okay.

(*She pushes him.*)

What was that for?

KATY: No reason.

COLIN: You're such a jerk.

KATY: (*smiling*) Yup. (*picking up her book*) So, this second law.

COLIN: Oh, here we go.

KATY: Now who's the jerk?

(*He shrugs. She pushes him again. He pushes her back. She jumps on him and starts tickling him. He laughs loudly. Fade to Black.*)

Scene 6

Late at night two weeks later. ROSS sits alone paging through the Air Force Academy brochure that Colin gave him earlier. He has his backpack from before next to him. He looks tired.

He gets to the end of the old and worn brochure and then stares at the cover for a while.

He puts a hand to his eyes and begins to cry.

He stops quickly and wipes his eyes. He looks to the river, then to the brochure. He holds it out and drops it into the river.

He reaches into his pocket and pulls out his pack of cigarette and his lighter. He takes out a cigarette and goes to light it, but stops and stares at it.

He hangs his head and throws the cigarette, the lighter, and the rest of the pack into the river.

He puts his hands in his pockets and discovers his cell phone. He takes it out and dials a number.

He lets it ring.

ROSS: (into the phone) Dad? ... Yeah, I'm home.

   (*Slow fade to black.*)

Scene 7

KATY and COLIN are sitting on the bridge that spring. Each holds two letters.

KATY: (*flipping the letters back and forth*) Which one should we open first?

COLIN: Neither. Let's throw them in the river and go home.

KATY: Sorry. Not an option. Which one? State or New York?

(*Colin looks at both the letters. Pause.*)

COLIN: Let's do State first. It's safer.

KATY: (*smiling*) Okay. State it is. Open together?

COLIN: Yeah.

KATY: (*preparing to rip hers*) Okay, ready?

COLIN: (*poised as well*) Ready.

KATY: One, two... three.

(*They rip them open and unfold the letters. They read. Silence. Colin looks at Katy. Katy looks at Colin.*)

COLIN: (*whispering*) I'm in. You?

KATY: Yeah.

COLIN: (*smiling*) Good. We aren't failures at life.

KATY: Yeah. Good.

(*Colin laughs.*)

Ready for the other one.

COLIN: (*getting up*) Nope. Let's skip it. We can go to Denny's instead. Celebrate State.

KATY: (*holding him down*) Colin.

COLIN: Okay, fine. Let's do it.

KATY: Let's. (*getting ready to rip her other envelope*) You ready?

COLIN: (*poised again*) No.

KATY: Yes you are.

COLIN: I know.

KATY: Okay. Here we go.

COLIN: Here we go.

KATY: One, two... three.

(*They rip them open and unfold the letters very quickly. They both read intently.*)

COLIN: (surprised) Katy.

KATY: What is it?

COLIN: I got in.

KATY: (*hugging him*) Colin! I knew you would!

COLIN: (*while being hugged*) What about you?

KATY: (*not letting him go*) I'm so proud of you.

COLIN: (*trying to break away from the hug*) Katy.

KATY: (*not giving in*) Colin.

COLIN: (*grabbing for it*) What did yours say.

KATY: (*pulling it away*) It doesn't matter. You got in.

COLIN: What about you?

KATY: (*moving away*) What does it matter?

COLIN : What are you talking about? Let me see your letter.

KATY: (*standing up*) No.

COLIN: (*standing up too*) Come on.

KATY: (*walking away*) No, Colin.

COLIN: (following her) Katy.

(*He grabs for the letter. She pulls it away. He grabs her wrist and takes the letter.*)

KATY: Colin. Don't.

(*He reads it. She walks away*)

COLIN: (*turning to Katy*) They didn't accept you.

KATY: I know.

COLIN: You didn't get in.

KATY: Yes, Colin. I didn't get in.

COLIN: This must be a mistake. You should have gotten in.

KATY: Colin, I just didn't make it.

COLIN: (*getting upset*) No. It's a mistake. You are supposed to get in. You're supposed to go with me.

KATY: Colin.

COLIN: (*yelling now*) No, Katy! Stop! You're going with me!

KATY: Colin. I didn't get in.

COLIN: You aren't leaving me!

KATY: Colin.

COLIN: (*starting to cry*) You aren't!

KATY: Look, Colin. I'm sorry.

COLIN: (*slumping to the ground*) I can't go by myself.

KATY: Now Colin.

COLIN: I can't. I won't.

KATY: Colin, you have to.

COLIN: No! I don't have to!

KATY: (*kneeling down next to him*) Yes, you do, Colin.

COLIN: (*looking up a her*) No. I'll stay here. We'll both go to State. It'll be fine.

KATY: You aren't giving this up.

COLIN: I'm not giving you up.

KATY: You're going to New York.

COLIN: I can't! I can't go without you! I won't make it!

KATY: Yes you will!

COLIN: No! I'm staying here! (crying now) I'll go to State. We'll go
together. We'll stay here. Right here. Together. Nothing will
change.

KATY: Colin. That's not what you want.

COLIN: It is!

KATY: It isn't.

COLIN: How do you know what I want?

KATY: Because I know. You need this. Don't you want to get out of
here? See the world?

COLIN: I can't do it by myself.

KATY: Yes, you can.

COLIN: I've been alone too long. Now I have you. I can't give you up.

KATY: You won't be. Look, Colin. You can do this. I believe in you.
(*Colin is audibly crying. He keeps shaking his head. Katy puts her
arms around him.*)
You'll be okay. Colin, listen to me. Listen.
(*He looks up at her.*)
You are the single most intelligent, wonderful, amazing boy, I've
ever met. You have so much to give the world. You're going to
really be something. You'll look back on this place and these
people and they will all be like, "I knew him when." But you'll be
beyond that. You'll be out there, making a name for yourself.
Whatever you choose to do, you will be the best.

COLIN: (*through tears*) I'm so scared.

KATY: That's okay. You're allowed to be. Everyone gets scared. Life
is pretty scary. But you'll make it. You know why?

COLIN: Why?

KATY: Because people do. People don't die from fear. People face that fear and overcome it. If you don't face it, it will always be there. It will always weigh you down. You're better than that. I know you're better than that, Colin. Do this. Put yourself out there. Take this chance. Life's a game. You can't sit and watch. You gotta play.

(*She wipes away one of his tears.*)

What do you say? Will you try?

(*He nods.*)

No regrets. 'kay?

(*He nods again.*)

(*holding out her pinky*) Pinky swear?

(*He smiles and holds out his. She takes it in hers.*)

COLIN: Pinky swear.

(*She laughs. He joins. Fade to black.*)

Scene 8

Night on the last day of summer, the bridge is empty. COLIN enters slowly. He looks around, runs his hand along the railing, and looks over the side of the bridge. He watches the river for a bit. He spits and watches it fall. He spits again.

COLIN: (*nodding*) Two seconds.

(*He spits again. ROSS enters. He stops when he sees Colin.*)

ROSS: (*quietly*) Colin.

(*Colin turns around.*)

COLIN: Ross?

ROSS: Your mom said you might be out here.

COLIN: Since when do you talk to my mother?

ROSS: Just today. I called. To talk to you. I heard you were going to New York.

COLIN: I am.

ROSS: Wow. That's pretty awesome. The big apple.

COLIN: Did you need something?

ROSS: I don't know.

COLIN: Why did you come here?

ROSS: I don't know.

(*Ross crosses to Colin. Silence. Colin spits.*)

(*watching the river*) Two seconds.

COLIN: Yeah. I know.

ROSS: Yeah.

(*Silence.*)

(*looking at Colin*) Colin.

(*Pause.*)

I want to apologize.

COLIN: For what?

ROSS: Everything.

COLIN: (*nonchalant*) Okay. You're forgiven.

ROSS: What?

COLIN: You're forgiven.

ROSS: I didn't apologize yet.

COLIN: Don't worry about it.

ROSS: Colin. I am worried about it.

COLIN: Don't. It's fine.

ROSS: No, it's not.

COLIN: Why not?

(*Pause.*)

ROSS: Because I was wrong. I wasn't a good friend. I screwed up, Colin.

COLIN: Ross, don't do this.

ROSS: You needed me, and I— I blew you off.

COLIN: (*a little forceful*) Ross, stop.

(*Silence.*)

I don't need you to tell me what you did. I was there. I'm over it. It's fine now. Everything is just fine.

ROSS: I just want to apologize.

COLIN: You did. It's okay.

ROSS: No, it's not. It's not okay. (he looks away) Did you hear that I
   went to California?

COLIN: Yeah. I heard you dropped out.

ROSS: I did. Stole my dad's car and went to California.
   (Beat.)
   But as soon as I got to the ocean I turned around. You know why?

COLIN: (not really interested) Why?

ROSS: Because I realized that I had messed everything up. I messed
   up my whole life. I messed up your life.

COLIN: You didn't.

ROSS: (upset) I did. You know I did. Don't say I didn't.

COLIN: You didn't, Ross. Things were bad for a bit, but I got through
   it. By myself. It turned out that I didn't need you.

ROSS: I know. But that doesn't make it right. The ends can't justify
   the means. I hurt you.

COLIN: You didn't.

ROSS: I did, Colin.

COLIN: Why are you bringing this up? I'm leaving for New York in the
   morning. I don't need this. Not now.

ROSS: I just need you to know that I'm sorry.
   (Silence.)
   (Colin goes to leave.)
   Don't you care? Stop walking away from me! We need to talk about
   this!

COLIN: No, Ross. You need to talk about this. I don't. I needed to
   talk about it three years ago when you left me all alone without a
   friend in the world. Where was your apology then? Where the fuck
   were you then?
   (He doesn't answer.)
   I know where. Passed out with your bitch of a girlfriend. Because
   you'd rather be unconscious then have to face reality and deal

with me.

(*Silence.*)

And, I'm not gonna lie. That hurt. It did. But it doesn't matter anymore. I'm past it. If you need me to forgive you so that you can clear your conscience, then fine, I forgive you, but I'm not about to take this trip down memory lane with you. Not now. Not tonight. You should have done this a long time ago. You've missed your chance.

(*Long Silence.*)

ROSS: Better late than never.

COLIN: No. Not really. Better never.

(*Colin goes to leave again.*)

ROSS: Colin.

(*Colin keeps going.*)

Colin! Stay!

(*Colin stops but doesn't turn around.*)

What do you say we just go get a bite to eat or something? My treat. A sort of farewell gift.

(*Colin turns.*)

COLIN: I'm not really that hungry.

(*He leaves. Ross is left alone. He spits into the river.*
Long fade to Black.)

END OF ACT TWO.

END OF PLAY.